Ros

FIBBY LIBBY

A GHOST ATE MY TOAST

Happy Cat Books
Published by Catnip Publishing Ltd.
14 Greville Street
London
EC1N 8SB

This edition published 2008
1 3 5 7 9 10 8 6 4 2

Text and illustrations copyright © 2008 Ros Asquith

A CIP catalogue record for this book is available from the British Library

ISBN 978-1-905117-63-5

Printed in Poland

www.catnippublishing.co.uk

CHAPTER ONE

Libby Normal was bored.

Her mother, Mrs Normal, her father, Mr Normal; and her teacher, Miss Wilderness, had told her, time and time again: 'There's no such word as "bored", do something useful for a change!'

Cloud of boredom

Whichever adult was talking to Libby at the time would then make a list of helpful suggestions:

Strange, Libby thought to herself on such occasions, what grown ups seem to find interesting . . .

But now, here she was, on the first day of the holidays, sitting in the grotty playground at the end of her very normal street in her extremely normal town, being bored.

Several of her school friends were there. Blonde sporty Barbara was doing backward somersaults in front of a small group of admirers.

GO ON!

Dark, skinny Yasmin was wiggling her ears at an amazed group of fans.

Brainy Billy King was reciting his fourteen times table while hanging by his toes off the highest bar of the climbing frame.

14 × 2 = 28
14 × 3 = 42

Libby hardly dared look. All around her,
children seemed to be having A Good Time.
Only Karen-next-door sat quietly on
the bench near Libby, looking down at her
brown sandals and humming softly.

hmmmmmm

Karen-next-door was perfectly nice,
thought Libby. But, well, dull. Like Libby
herself. They were both just ... so ...
normal.

Mrs Normal called that it was time to go home. Then she said something else.

Something slightly unusual.

'Guess what?' said Mrs Normal.

'We're having ham and boiled potatoes and frozen peas for tea?' said Libby.

'Yes – and something else.'

'Apple pie and lumpy custard?' sighed Libby.

'Well, yes,' murmured her mother. 'But there's something else – not to do with food.'

Hmmm ... not to do with food, thought Libby. 'Are we going the long way home so that you can look at that dress in the window of *Plumpo Fashions for the Mature-but-Young-at-Heart*?'

'Yes. But it's something else.'
Libby tried the usual options:

Picking up the dry
cleaning.

WHOOPS

Going to the
post office.

Buying a
How to Do It
magazine for her
father.

(He was feeling very low because he had
lost his job at the doughnut factory three
whole months ago and had still not found
another.)

'None of those,' said her mother smugly.
They were now outside *Plumpo Fashions*
and Mrs Normal was just wondering if she
could pour herself
into the daffodil
yellow dress
covered in puce
circles displayed in
the window. Sadly
she realised that
the dress was:
a) too expensive
and
b) three sizes too
small (despite
being marked
'Extra Large').

'I give up,' said Libby.
Mrs Normal came out of her daydream
and smiled as brightly as her mood allowed.
'Well. You've had an invitation.'

Libby's heart thumped. Not a party. Please, please, please, not a party. She never knew what to wear to parties. If she wore her party dress, all the other girls were in leggings and roller blades. If she wore her leggings and plimsolls (Mrs Normal disapproved of trainers) then all the other girls would be in ribbons and petticoats . . .

And she *hated* games. She had never even been able to Pass the Parcel without dropping it or tearing off two lots of paper instead of one.

'Oh no! Not a party!' she squeaked.

'Not a party,' agreed Mrs Normal.

Then what? Before Libby had time to imagine any more horrors, Mrs Normal filled the void: 'Your Aunty Cora has invited you to stay at The Castle for a week! And to go to the Country Show! Won't that be wonderful! Aren't you lucky?'

Libby was so used to her mother saying how wonderful things were and how lucky she was, when all she was talking about was that the frozen peas weren't soggy, or that there was butter on the potatoes, that at first she didn't take in what her mother had just said.

Then she did.

CHAPTER TWO

Libby was, in fact, overjoyed. Aunt Cora!
The mysterious, magical Aunt Cora, who
had arrived in Libby's life for the first (and,
so far, only) time last year with her arms
full of a Spanish flamenco dancer's dress!

Aunt Cora, who, despite being Mr
Normal's sister, looked nothing like him at all.
She had long black hair and red lipstick and
lived, Libby had just discovered, in a castle!
And she was going to take her to a show!

Libby's mother had gone on to say that
Aunt Cora would be showing Kew Kumba,
which was obviously the name of her
show-jumper! She probably had a whole
stable-full of horses!

Maybe Libby would be allowed to ride them – and even enter a competition!

She couldn't wait to run and tell Karen-next-door all about it. So, directly after she had finished her ham, potatoes, frozen peas, burnt apple pie and lumpy custard, she rang Karen-next-door's bell.

'She's got a castle!' shouted Libby.

'A castle!' whispered Karen. 'Maybe there'll be a ghost!'

Libby went quiet. 'Oh, I don't believe in ghosts.'

But she did. And she was worried.

★ ★ ★

Libby told everyone about her forthcoming visit, adding to the details as she went along, to ... well, to keep her courage up.

'Apparently the castle's got the highest turret in the whole of the British Isles,' she told Billy King.

'So?' said Billy King. 'Not as high as a mountain, eh? And I'll be seeing *plenty* of those on my climbing holiday.'

Libby *hated* it when he said 'So?' in that know-all way. 'It's got the deepest moat, too,' she said wildly.

'You can still get more water in the sea! And I'll see *plenty* of that in Majorca,' boasted Yasmin, wiggling her ears furiously.

'She owns more horses than anyone except the Queen!'

'Nah!' sneered Barbara, somersaulting backwards past Libby's left ear.

17

'There's some sheik who owns far more. My dad told me. He *knows* about racing. He's going to take me to the racing stables near Bognor.'

'She – she's got an antique car!'

'You can't have antique *cars*,' jeered everyone at once.

In desperation, Libby cried: 'Well, there's a GHOST! With chains, and whooooing noises – and no HEAD!'

 Yasmin's ears went very pale.

 Barbara looked as though she might cry.

Billy King went the teeniest bit green.

'Bet there isn't,' he gulped. 'Ghosts like that only happen in STORIES.'

'Well, you wait and see,' said Libby. 'Wait and see. I'll write to you ALL about it.'

CHAPTER THREE

On Wednesday afternoon, Libby's mother took her to Aunt Cora's. Aunt Cora, black hair flowing down her back, was waiting at the coach station. Libby looked around eagerly for the antique car her dad was always going on about – but all she could see was a beat up old Morris Minor.

'Yup. Centuries old, but I love it,' said Aunt Cora cheerfully, whisking Libby in among a lot of old rugs covered in cabbage leaves and mud. Probably just uses it for short trips, thought Libby, blushing as she listened to her mother's list of instructions.

'Please don't keep her up late, Cora. Remember she must wrap up warmly, she's very prone to chills and terribly . . .' At this point Mrs Normal lowered her voice and whispered in Cora's ear for about five minutes. What *was* she saying? Surely Libby wasn't that hopeless? *Was* she? Suddenly Libby felt very homesick indeed. She wished she could be back in her nice normal house with its comforting flowery wallpaper, instead of going off to a creaky old castle . . . She gazed at the distant turrets with a feeling of deep foreboding.

Libby was surprised to find, five minutes later, that her aunt was not driving towards the huge castle in the distance, but was, instead, pulling up in front of a small semi-detached cottage, with roses round the door and a neat lawn full of gnomes.

'Aren't we going to the castle?'

'Oh, of course we'll visit it,' said Aunt Cora, 'but I thought you'd like to settle in first.'

The truth dawned slowly on Libby. Little things, like her aunt taking out keys and opening the cottage door,

picking up the post,
hanging up her coat.
So *this* was her aunt's
house. But perhaps – a
faint glimmer of hope

– it was just one of many cottages in the
castle grounds, and Aunt Cora owned them
all.

But Libby couldn't kid herself about this
for long, because just then she noticed the
name on the cottage door . . .

'The Castle', indeed! What a daft name for a cottage. What a fool Libby felt!

Still, she had the horse show to look forward to. Obviously Kew Kumba and her aunt's other horses must be in stables somewhere, because all she could see from the cottage window was a neat patch of lawn, a vegetable plot and a potting shed. Not even Libby could imagine a show-jumper squeezed into a potting shed!

'Cheer up!' said Aunt Cora, taking pity on her little round niece, who reminded her of a currant bun, 'We'll visit the castle straight away if you like!'

That evening, Libby borrowed some of her aunt's notepaper . . .

CHAPTER FOUR

The Castle
Little Cowpat
HERTS

Dear Yasmin,
    The castle is REALLY
spooooky. It has got 400 rooms
but 401 windows!!!! So
WHERE is the other room?!
No one has ever found it!!
There are 206 suits of
armour and 48 stags heads
with ENORMOUS antlers
It is freezing cold, colder
than an iceberg.
    I haven't seen the ghost
— yet!
    Love,
                Libby

That night, Libby was very relieved that
she *wasn't* staying in the creepy old castle
at the top of the village. She was happy to
curl up with some hot chocolate and a hot
water bottle in her aunt's spare bedroom
with the flowery wallpaper very like the
one they had at home. Aunt Cora had even
been kind enough to let her borrow her
old teddy – and Libby drifted happily off
to sleep, dreaming of the Country Show in
three day's time.

BUT

what seemed like only seconds later, Libby woke up with her heart racing.

The room was pitch black. What was that horrible, gruesome sound?

Diving under the bedclothes, Libby screamed.

The sound was joined by another. A creaking, clanking, groaning gurgle. It was the ghost! It could only be the ghost! Libby could hear its wail. She could hear it dragging its chains up the stairs. It got louder and louder. It was outside her door!

Shivering with terror, she huddled deeper into her bed.

Silence.

Slowly, very slowly, she reached out her arm and fumbled for the bedside light. Once she had switched it on, she had the courage to peep out.

Everything looked normal. Had it been a dream?

THEN

the noise started again.

Whooooo CLANK
CLANK gurgle
WHO-O-O-Eeek

Libby screamed and screamed and
screamed.

'Whatever's the
matter?' Her aunt raced
in, frantic.

'The ghost, the
ghost! Listen!'

Aunt Cora was baffled.

'Listen!' screamed Libby.

'Oh *that*! It's just the
old central heating boiler,
warming up for the morning. You
poor thing! No more visits to castles for
you!'

The Castle
Little Cowpat
HERTS

Dear Karen,
        Last night I heard the most **SCARY** sounds I have ever heard! HOWLS, **WAILS** and the CLANKING of chains! I leapt out of bed to save my aunt. Suddenly the noise stopped! When I turned round there was a HAIRY CREATURE in my bed!!! Kind of **MOTH-EATEN** with only one arm. And no **EYES!**
        How will I survive a whole WEEK? If you never see me again you can have my special Easter Egg that I've been saving (it's not **THAT** mouldy) and my Pony books.
        yours in **TERROR**
                        Libby

Libby gazed at her aunt's eyeless, one armed old teddy as she licked the envelope and smiled to herself.

CHAPTER FIVE

The next day Libby plucked up courage to ask her aunt about the horses. Where were they kept, could she perhaps have a ride?

'Horses? Who said I had horses?' laughed Cora.

'D–Dad, M–Mum, Y–You!' blurted Libby. 'Y-you all said you'd take me to the show, and you were showing Kew Kumba . . .'

Aunt Cora was laughing so much she could hardly speak. Then she saw the tears in Libby's eyes. 'Oh dear. No castle, no ghost. And now no horse. We *are* going to the Country Show. But it's a flower and vegetable show, not a horse show. I'm showing my prize cucumbers!'

Libby sobbed.

'There might be pony rides,' added her aunt kindly.

Dear Yasmin,

I have got used to the
WAILS and **CLANKING** and
the **FURRY BEAST** and now
I sleep quite soundly.
It is lucky, I suppose,
that I have such a ~~sora conf~~
~~conf~~ courageous nature.
The Country Show is
tomorrow and I am sure that
Kew-Kumba will win FirstPrize!
I may be allowed to ride myself!!

As you know, I have a natural
ability at such things.
Hope Majorca isn't too HOT—
I'd be bored stiff all day
just on a beach.

Cheers!!

Libby

To her surprise, Libby enjoyed spending the whole day helping her aunt with her prize vegetables. Cucumbers were Aunt Cora's pride and joy and they certainly were magnificent. But Aunt Cora was also entering a marrow and some beautiful golden daisies, almost as big as sunflowers.

By tea time, Libby and Aunt Cora were aching all over and caked in mud. Aunt

Cora looked like a marsh monster and they
had fun pretending to be Creatures from
the Swamp. Libby had never met an adult
who would do childish things like that. It
was a luxury to soak in a hot bath and
have crumpets with strawberry jam. Libby
wondered whether she could persuade her
mother to dare to try a crumpet instead of
Wreckyerbelly white sliced loaf . . .

The Castle

Little Cowpat

HERT'S

Dear Karen,

We spent all day getting ready for the show. I saw a long skinny **THING** with jet Black HAIR, covered in gooey **SLIME** in the garden.

I suppose it was the famed HERTFORDSHIRE **CREATURE FROM THE SWAMP...**

I now hope to show Daisy tomorrow. Daisy is the most gorgeous colour—gold!

I **THINK** gold horses are called palomino.

Hope the rain didn't spoil your day in the Theme Park. I heard the queues were three hours long.

yours **EERILY**
Libby xx

Libby was keeping her spirits up surprisingly well by writing her letters, but secretly she felt bitterly disappointed about the castle and the horses. She wasn't sure she could convince Karen and the others that she'd actually *ridden* on a bunch of flowers and vegetables without, well, *lying*. (Which, she told herself, she had not done – so far . . .)

CHAPTER SIX

The next morning Aunt Cora and Libby
were up at the crack of dawn.

Aunt Cora treated her vegetables like
children. 'There now, darling,' she murmured
tenderly to her marrow, as she laid it,
wrapped in a rainbow wool blanket, on the
back seat of the antique car.

'Do your best for me,' she whispered to
the cucumbers. 'Shine for Libby,' she smiled
at the daisies, stroking their petals ever so
gently.

Libby's heart swelled. She *was* going to be
allowed to show the daisies then.

The Castle
Little Cowpat
HERTS

Dear Barbara,
   Today is the Big Day. I am showing Daisy at the Country Show. I am very nervous. What if the **GHOST** or the Creature from the **SWAMP** turn up and spook the animals? Or I fall in the moat?
   Sorry to hear you were disqualified from the somersaulting competition in Bognor. And sorry your Dad made a mistake about the racehorses. I heard from Karen they were seaside donkeys....
   Wish me luck with Daisy!
Love,
      Libby

When they arrived at the show, the village green was covered in marquees. The dark sky promised dreadful weather, but there was already a large crowd of competitors although it was only 7.30 am. There *were* pony rides!

And Aunt Cora promised Libby she could have one after the judging. The ponies were little brown Shetlands. Very sweet, but a bit babyish, thought Libby. Still, she would be able, honestly, to tell Karen she had ridden . . .

Libby and Aunt Cora took a lot of time arranging the daisies and cucumbers. Libby spent ages poking the stems of the daisies through holes in a little upside-down sieve, so they would stand up proudly with just their heads nodding down.

She chose grasses and leaves to surround them and wondered whether she might be rather artistic after all.

'Gorgeous,' enthused Aunt Cora, giving her largest cucumber a hearty polish. 'You could earn a fortune as a florist.'

Libby's heart sank. She had been enjoying herself up until now. But suddenly her future shrank. Not a show-jumper, or a film star, or a world famous ghost-buster. Possibly a nice normal job at the local flower shop.

'You've got a face like a wet Wednesday.' Her aunt's voice cut into her daydream. 'The judges like to see a smile, you know.'

Libby tried to cheer up, but looking round the marquee she knew they hadn't a hope of winning. Look at those carrots! And marigolds! And posh roses! And amazing cabbages, the size of bean bags!

At that moment there was the most fantastic din. The storm broke, thunder crashed and rolled, lightning flashed and the little row of brown Shetland ponies broke their ropes in terror and galloped into the marquee! It was chaos.

One pony stopped to nibble the giant carrots. Another buried its nose happily in some turnips. A third made short work of some marigolds. The fourth trampled cabbages, roses and Lady Trump-Merrily's famed display of lilies and irises.

Libby whisked her precious daisies — and herself — under the table. All she could see were legs, hooves, and the prone form of Lady Trump-Merrily, who had fainted at the sight of her adorable lilies disappearing into the mouth of a hairy four-footed creature. The ponies chomped their way through most of the exhibits. The poor girl who was supposed to be in charge of pony rides sat on the ground and wept.

'Oats and sugar!' cried Aunt Cora. 'The only thing that will get them out is oats and sugar.'

The girl in charge of pony rides saw a glimmer of hope. She blew her nose fiercely on her sleeve and went off to her cart, returning with a sack of oats and a bag of sugar lumps. The ponies, by now full of flowers, fruit and veg, were calmer and quite fancied oat and sugar lump pudding to round off their tea.

They left the tent as meek as lambs, leaving devastation in their wake.

Meanwhile, Lady Trump-Merrily was being revived with brandy by the vet.

The vicar's wife, whose entire vegetable plot had been trampled to dust, was on her knees attempting to rescue her one remaining parsnip from the hands of a roving toddler.

And grown men wept at the sight of their perfect produce, half-eaten and drooping.

The judges, however, continued their slow progress round the tent.

'Courage,' they murmured to the exhibitors. 'Be brave! We can see you did a grand job,' they said, kindly, to a trio of old ladies who now only had a mangled turnip and two pea pods to show for all their hard work.

Aunt Cora, regarded as Saving The Day with her quick thinking, stood proudly by her cucumbers and her marrow. She had stuffed the marrow up her jumper and, as

luck would have it, the ponies seemed not to have been keen on salad. The only other surviving produce was some not very fine lettuce. And, of course, Libby's daisies, or to be more precise, daisy, which appeared, followed by Libby, from under the marquee table, just as the judges passed.

Sadly, she had only been able to rescue one from the hubbub. But it was the *ONLY* flower left in the flower section.

'What an excellent daisy.'

'Beautiful colour.'

'Fine arrangement.' (There were still a few grasses surrounding the flower.)

The daisy won first prize in the flower section. The cucumbers won first prize in the vegetable section, with the marrow second and the not-very-fine lettuce third.

Libby was awarded a magnificent red rosette and a certificate that read:

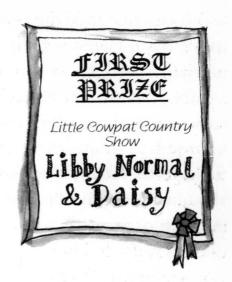

FIRST PRIZE

Little Cowpat Country Show

Libby Normal & Daisy

The last bit was hand lettered in italics – and Libby's only complaint was that she failed to get the judge to write '*for Show-jumping*' afterwards.

Aunt Cora made a very kind little speech about how she didn't deserve to win and how very sorry she was for Lady Trump-Merrily (who now looked very merry after rather too much brandy). She also thanked the vicar's wife and all the other people who had worked so hard to make the show a success. This made everyone happy and made them feel that they were splendid people.

Libby and Aunt Cora went out into the sunshine to thank the ponies. The girl in charge was so grateful to Aunt Cora for her idea about the oats and sugar lumps that she gave Libby a free ride on every pony! All four of them!

CHAPTER SEVEN

The Castle
Little Cowpat
HERTS

Dear Barbara,
The show was just amazing!
Daisy and I won FIRST PRIZE!
Aunty Cora won first prize with
Kew-Kumba in the other class and
second prize too! Some of the
ponies went crazy and Lady
Trump-Merrily (who owns half
the village, but not the CASTLE, of
course) fainted!
I'm going to ride every day
till I get back.
REALLY sorry about Bognor.

Cheers,   Libby

The Castle
Little Cowpat
HERTS

Dear Yasmin,
        Kew-Kumba **AND** Daisy
BOTH won first prizes!
I showed Daisy!!
        REALLY sorry to hear
from Karen about your
sunburn — I didn't know you
could get it on your **EARS**.
        All the best, Libby

The Castle
Little Cowpat
HERTS

Dear Billy,
        Hope you don't mind me
writing, but I had to tell you
I'm not scared of **GHOSTS**
any more.
        There was a **HAIRY THING**
without EYES in my bed the night I

arrived! I heard WAILS and CLANKS all night! Then I saw the Creature from the SWAMP in the garden. THEN at the Country Show, **FOUR HAIRY** creatures oozing mud with BLazing eyes and HOOVES instead of hands attacked the flower and vegetable tent!

There were rumblings like thunder and blinding flashes of light and people were screaming and **FAINTING**. I admit I hid under a table for a short while but **THEN** I went onto win **FIRST PRIZE** with Daisy. I bet you won't read about it in the papers, because they always hush up things like this.

Sorry to hear you broke your leg climbing. Still I bet you've learnt your 19 times table by now. See you next term.

From

Libby

Libby was very pleased with this last letter. Now she could relax and enjoy the next few days, riding the Shetland ponies and helping her aunt in the garden.

BUT

Just two days later her Aunt Cora exclaimed, 'How nice. A letter from your mum.'

After reading it, a funny look came into Aunt Cora's eye. 'Mmmmmm. Would you like to read this, Libby?' she asked, her voice a shade deeper than usual.

Libby gulped. She could tell something was wrong. But what? Trembling, she took the letter.

2 Dreary St,
Normalton,
Bleak-on-the-Common,
Dullsville.

My dear Cora,

I am most disturbed to hear of strange goings on at the Castle.

Several of Libby's friends, including dear little Karen-next-door, who NEVER fibs, have told me that Libby has been woken by ghosts, seen a creature from a swamp, won a show-jumping competition and, horror of horrors, shared a bed with a monster (!!!!).

The latest news has come from that very clever little boy Billy King, who says Libby has gone quite mad and believes four wild creatures attacked the fruit and vegetable marquee, emitting laser rays as they did so! I know that Libby's imagination, as I told you, runs away with her, but I beg you to put my mind at rest about these goings on.

If only, dear Cora, you were on the phone! I haven't dared mention these things to Libby's father, he is depressed enough as it is.

Yours, desperately worried,
Betty.

Libby read this with mounting despair. How could she have been so silly? Now her poor mother was going mad with worry. She wished she was back in her nice normal house in her nice normal street and that she had never set eyes on the castle or the Country Show or Aunt Cora or anything.

She burst into tears and ran out of the house to lock herself in the potting shed. Her Aunt Cora did not follow to bang on the door. Nobody came. The potting shed smelled of old cats. It was dark. Outside, the wind howled. Something creaked. Something banged. Libby crouched, miserable and scared, for what seemed like hours.

In fact, it was only minutes later that Aunt Cora came to look for her, found her sobbing among the flower pots, sat her down at the kitchen table and asked for an explanation.

CHAPTER EIGHT

Half an hour later, Aunt Cora went down to the village phone box and reassured Libby's mother. She told her the whole truth, but very kindly added that she would write a letter explaining everything (leaving some things out) and that Libby could show it to her friends.

And this is the letter that Aunt Cora wrote.

The Castle
Little Cowpat
Herts

To whom it may concern:

The castle DOES have 400 rooms and 401 windows. (*This was the castle at the top of the village, of course.*)

There WERE howls, wails and clankings on the first two nights that Libby stayed here.

There WAS something hairy without eyes and with only one arm in her bed.

She DID see a long thin thing with jet black hair covered in mud in the garden.

There WERE sounds like thunder and flashes like lightning at the Country Show.

Four wild muddy creatures with hooves DID enter the tent (although they did not emit laser rays, that is Billy King's imagination at work).

Lady Trump-Merrily DOES own half the village and she DID faint.

Libby DID ride four ponies.

Libby DID win first prize at the Country Show with Daisy, and she has the certificate and the rosette to prove it.

Signed

Cora Normal.

Libby certainly didn't feel normal any more. She knew she was incredibly lucky to have such a kind, thoughtful aunt and such an adorable mother, who wouldn't give her away. She could show all her friends the rosette, the certificate, and Aunt Cora's letter.

The first person she showed them to was Karen, who looked very impressed, then very thoughtful. 'Those four wild things with hooves weren't PONIES, were they?' she asked innocently. 'And that thing without eyes in your bed sounds very like a teddy . . .'

She saw Libby's face fall. She had been going on to say that things covered in mud in gardens were usually gardeners and that Kew Kumba sounded very like a vegetable to her.

But Libby's expression stopped her.

'Gosh, you were BRAVE,' said Karen.
'And you,' said Libby, 'are my best friend.'